HANNAH'S
Collections

MARTHE JOCELYN

Dutton Children's Books
NEW YORK

FOR NELL,
THE REAL COLLECTOR

CIP Data is available.

Published in the United States 2000 by Dutton Children's Books,
a division of Penguin Putnam Books for Young Readers
345 Hudson Street, New York, New York 10014
www.penguinputnam.com
Designed by Sara Reynolds
Photography by Sandi Fellman and Doug Keljikian
Printed in Hong Kong • First Edition
ISBN 0-525-46442-5
1 3 5 7 9 10 8 6 4 2

The art for this book was done in mixed-media collage, using cloth, paper, yarn,
plastic, feathers, wood, glass, metal, rubber, and found objects.

Hannah loved to collect things.
She found new treasures wherever she went.

Her room was starting to look like a museum!

When her teacher made an announcement one Friday, asking the children to bring in a collection to share with the class, Hannah was a bit worried. How could she choose just one collection to bring to school? Every collection was her favorite.

Hannah had more buttons than anything else. She had 153 buttons. She counted them every time she found a new one. She sorted them in cupcake tins, sometimes by size, sometimes by shape, sometimes by color.

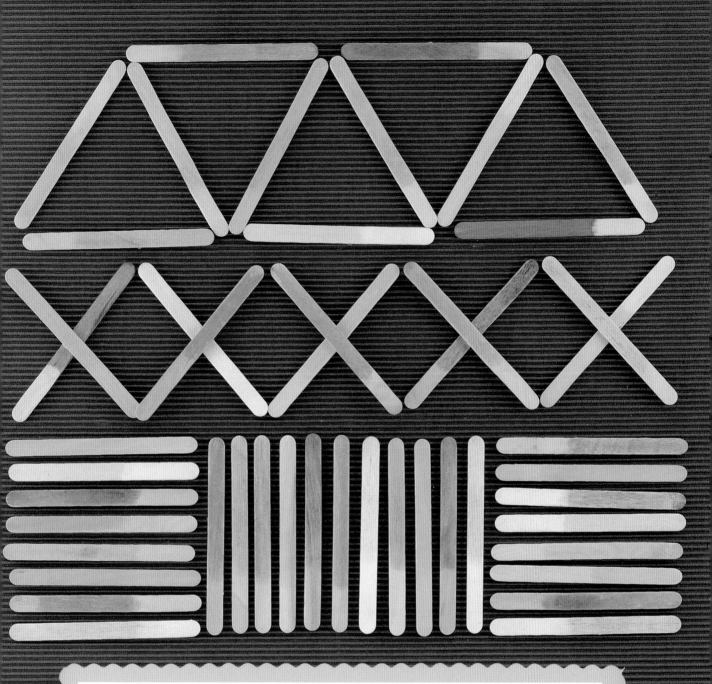

Since she had started collecting, Hannah had eaten many Popsicles and saved all the sticks. She arranged them in patterns of triangles, X's, and lines.

Hannah also found things with their own patterns from nature.

She had picked up **43** seashells on the beach last summer, and each had a different design. So did the shell of her pet turtle, Davey.

Hannah's 19 feathers had spots and speckles and stripes. Her 10 leaves had crisscrosses and curves and points.

Hannah chose barrettes with matching designs for Ellie. She could never decide if she had 14 barrettes or 7 pairs of barrettes. But when she and Ellie got dressed up, they looked very fancy indeed.

Altogether, Hannah had two dozen little creatures. She let Ellie look after the elephant family, who lived in the chocolate box. The others stood in a row along her shelf, lined up from the tallest to the smallest.

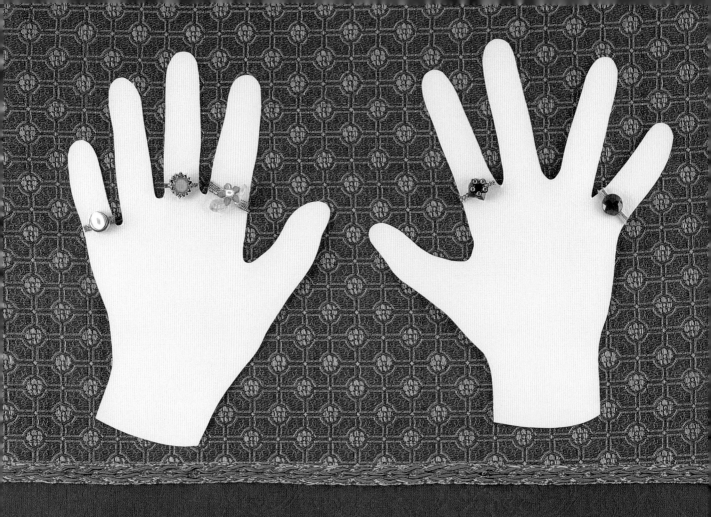

Hannah also collected jewelry. She had 5 rings. Sometimes she wore all of them on one hand. Or she might wear 4 on one hand and 1 on the other. Or 3 on one hand and 2 on the other.

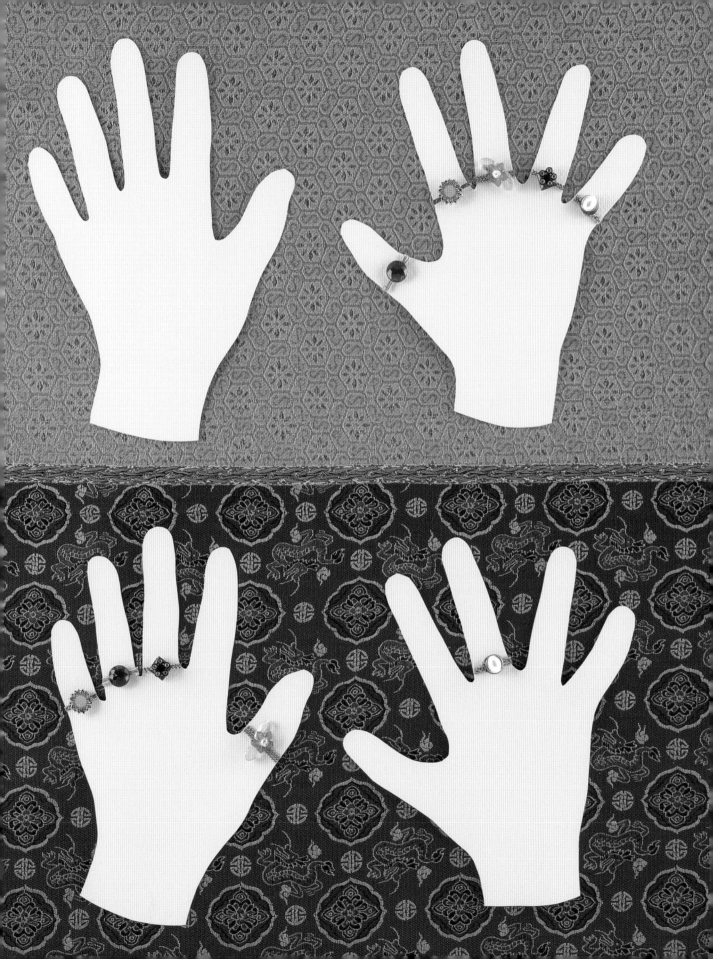

And Hannah had still more collections to choose from! Which one should she take to school?

Hannah thought and thought. Finally, she pressed her fists against her eyes until she saw fireworks. Then she had an idea that would solve everything.

She borrowed a tray from the kitchen. She found the glue bottle in the cupboard. She gathered up sticky tape and thumbtacks and cardboard and string and rubber bands.

She needed a lot of buttons, some feathers, a couple of leaves, several seashells, a few little creatures, and most of her Popsicle sticks.

She used 10 coins from Uncle Matthew's travels,

9 special erasers,

CANADA

8 keys that didn't lock things anymore,

7 stamps from faraway places,

6 pieces of striped candy,

5 clothespins that she kept in a polka-dot bag,

4 fake ladybugs,

3 miniature books,

and 2 weird wallets.

Hannah worked all weekend on her smart idea.

"And now," said Hannah on Monday, "I have one thing to take to school! It's the first piece in my new sculpture collection!"